THE THREE COWS THAT DIDN'T BECOME HAMBURGER

by Robert Harris

Illustrations by Maren Scott

Robert D. Harris
P.O. Box 3309
Logan, Utah 84323-3309
(435)787-1078

The paintings in this book were done in watercolor and color pencil.
The text type was set in Cheltenham

Book manufactured by Hiller Industries
Salt Lake City, Utah

Printed in the United States of America
First Edition

ISBN: 1-56713-123-9
Library of Congress Catalog Card Number: Applied for.
UPC 633356 70903 9

THE THREE COWS THAT DIDN'T BECOME HAMBURGER
by Robert Harris

Illustrations by Maren Scott

To Terri—my wife, inspiration and best friend.

Robert D. Harris

For my mother, my friend.

Maren Scott

THE THREE COWS THAT DIDN'T BECOME HAMBURGER

The bottom lands of the Logan Valley had always been a magical place for children. A tree-lined, muddy-banked river snaked its way slowly through the meadows and farmlands, acting as if it had nowhere to go and all day to get there. Thick willow patches and velvet grass stood tall and still, shimmering in the hot afternoon sun.

As the shiny blue pick-up truck came to a stop, the door flew open, the children bailed out, and the race was on for the river! Even though he was bigger and faster, Blake never got there first. Little Haddie darted under the willows, never slowing down, not even for a snagged pigtail.

Everything that floated around the river bend became instantly doomed—leaves, sticks, and even unfortunate floating insects. Turning to pick up another rock, Blake had a fleeting glance of what looked like three black and white shadows slipping into a large patch of berry bushes. He stared, rubbed his eyes, shook his head and then continued the serious job of sinking the enemy's navy.

Sensing that someone or something was watching her, Haddie swung around several times, but all she saw were rustling bushes. "Probably just birds stealing berries," she thought.

When the clammy steam hit the back of her neck, her knees went weak and her face went white. But her mouth still worked. She turned and made a most remarkable piercing and irritating scream. Better, in fact, than the ones that often got her sent to her room. Even better than the ones that made neighbor kids line up glasses to see if she could break them.

Blake and Haddie were now standing face to face with six large bloodshot eyes and two tons of angry cow! The three black and white cows threw dirt with their feet and shot steam from their nostrils.

Gently and carefully, Haddie placed her hand on one of the cow's heads and started to scratch. Blake did the same. The cows quit kicking dirt and blowing steam. Big round tears ran down their large faces, making little splats in the dust as they fell to the ground.

A sputtering, rattling clang echoed from across the meadow. Little smoke donuts puffed into the air. An old red rusty truck with a wooden rack on the back bounced toward the children. The cows began to blow steam and kick dust. Blake's heart missed a beat as he read the sign on the side of the truck:

FARMER DON'S BEEF AND HAMBURGER

Today was the day Farmer Don was taking the three cows to the butcher. But the cows had escaped from the corral and were on their way to hide in the mountains. They were determined to trample anyone who got in their way. After all, the cows thought that people only liked them because they could make hamburger out of them.

Sparkles in the children's eyes and gentle smiles surprised the cows. Could these two people be different?

While the three cows lay perfectly still, Blake and Haddie quickly covered them with grass, bushes and leaves. All that showed of the cows were three pretty pink noses that looked like perfectly planted petunias.

Farmer Don swung the door open and stumbled from his truck. Tall and skinny, tan and leathery, he towered over the children. The seat of his worn-out blue jeans hung almost to his knees. His red and white plaid shirt was dirty and his yellow straw hat looked like chickens had been roosting in it. As he chewed on a fat, short, unlit cigar, he drawled, "Ya kids seen ma cows?"

It became so silent Haddie could hear the petunias breathing.

"Cat got yer tongue, kids?" grumbled the farmer.

Frozen in place, Blake raised his little arm and pointed across the river toward the mountains. Saying nothing else, the farmer straightened his pants, moved the cigar to the corner of his mouth, and spat at one of the petunias. Getting back into his truck, he rattled down along the river bank and across the old wooden bridge. Leaving a trail of little smoke donuts, Farmer Don's truck disappeared into the trees.

The cows crawled out of their hiding place. As a stiff breeze blew across the river and the sun dropped behind the large mountains to the west, Blake and Haddie stared at the three doomed cows huddled together on the river bank. Blake got a knot in his stomach, and Haddie felt a lump growing in her throat. The cows' tails spun in nervous circles as Haddie blurted out, "Come on! You're coming home with us!"

The odd group stayed in the willow patches and tall grass as they wound their way from the river to Dad's truck.

As dusk settled over the meadow, Dad hiked up the trail from his favorite fishing spot. He stopped with a jolt as he saw three big black and white cows sitting calmly and comfortably in the back of his truck. As Dad walked past the cows to open the door, they turned their heads and smiled in unison. Dad had never seen cows smile before and was amazed at their huge teeth!

It was dark before Blake and Haddie told their dad the story of what had happened enough times that he believed it. Dad kept turning around and looking at the cows through the window. The cows kept smiling!

Maybe it was their great emotion, or maybe their many tears, but, "On a trial basis," Dad said, "the cows can come home!"

Trustingly, the cows lay down in the back of the truck, and Dad covered them with clean straw. The three cows and the three humans felt a little odd as they headed for the large house on the hill.

Driving towards town, Dad's heart pounded as he saw Farmer Don's Beef and Hamburger truck shadowed from the moonlight under a large oak tree. A tall skinny man in the middle of the road waved his hat.

"Eve'nin!" said the farmer.

"Good evening!" replied the children's father.

"Cute young-uns ya got there. Lookin' fer ma cows, mister!" growled the farmer.

"Well, good luck, sir," Father replied, as he drove slowly away.

As the truck pulled down the gravel lane, the farmer threw his cigar to the ground and stared at a big shiny hoof sticking out of the straw and glistening in the moonlight!

It's just too scary to tell you what happened when they all got home and told the long story to their mom. But the cows kept smiling. Dad kept smiling right along with the cows. And the kids did a lot of fast talking.

The cows were given a bucket of water, fed three whole boxes of cereal, and put to bed under the apple trees on the lawn. The kids went to bed without complaining, and Dad and Mom retired to their room.

Putting their ears right against the door, Blake and Haddie didn't like what they heard. Mom said, "They'll mess on the lawn and eat all the roses."

And Dad said, "I hate those big smiles and pink runny noses!"

The kids had to prove to their parents that cows were helpful creatures with feelings and emotions—that they were good for something more than hamburger.

Quietly, Blake and Haddie got dressed, tiptoed down the stairs and outside for a very important meeting with the cows!

The sun was just starting to shine through the window as Dad and Mom woke up. But it wasn't the sun that woke them, it was the noise. Hearing a loud chattering sound, they went to the window and stared outside in disbelief!

There on the lawn of the estate were two cows lined up side by side with Haddie holding a guiding tail in each hand. Their enormous teeth chattered rapidly as they mowed the lawn to the perfect height in straight rows. They were both wearing big white diapers.

Walking out of their bedroom, Dad and Mom froze—half in fear and half in amazement. They watched a long pink slippery tongue clean the top crystals of the chandelier that the cleaning people had never been able to reach! Standing on the tips of her hind hooves and stretching her fat neck as far as she could, one of the cows was just finishing her work. The house had been cleaned, dusted, and vacuumed.

A fresh pitcher of milk and a jar of creamy butter had been neatly placed on the front porch!

Tears were shed, the cows were fed, and Blake and Haddie jumped up and down on the bed. The cows were home to stay! Dad even told the cows they could quit smiling all the time.

Dad, Mom and the three cows stood at the gate as the children left for school. When the gate opened, chills went up and down their spines. Puffy little smoke donuts were rising above the house tops. There was a line of them stretching from the farmlands. Suddenly, Farmer Don's Beef and Hamburger truck shot around the corner and rattled to a stop right in front of the gate.

Nothing the children said helped. Farmer Don wanted his cows, and he insisted they leave NOW! Dad and Mom watched but did nothing as the cows were loaded into the rusty old red truck. Dad knew the cows were looking at him, but they weren't smiling anymore. Their large lazy ears flapped in the wind as they drove away from the house.

Dad and Mom hung their heads and went back into the house. The kids left for school.

Blake and Haddie coasted down the hill on their bikes. Smoke donuts kept hitting them in the face. Staying a safe distance behind, they followed the truck through town. It stopped at a dirty old smelly place on the outskirts of town. A big sign read, "LOGAN STOCKYARDS."

This was the last stop for the cows before the hamburger factory. Farmer Don got out of his truck and tried to unload the cows, but they clung to the wooden rack of the truck with their teeth.

He tugged on their tails.
He hung on their horns.
He pushed with his boots
on the ends of their snoots.
But he couldn't budge the big brutes.

He jabbed and he jerked. He pulled and he pushed. But it did no good.

Just as the cows thought they were out of luck, Blake and Haddie jumped into the front of the truck. Short little Haddie stood on the seat, and Blake lay on the floor and pushed on the gas with his feet. Haddie started the truck, and Farmer Don did a backwards somersault landing face first in the muck.

As the truck sped away from the stockyards, the three cows hung over the wooden rail and made disgusting faces at Farmer Don. The kids were amazed at the cows' **long** tongues!

The truck hit a rock and a tire went "BANG!" And thus began quite a sight for the stockyard gang. Everyone watched as Farmer Don ran down the gravel road. Because of his boots and his baggy pants, he scurried down the road in a backwards-leaning prance. But he wasn't slow—he had cows to catch and places to go!

Blake and Haddie jumped out of the truck and ran down the road toward town. But they were no match for skinny, long-legged Farmer Don. Suddenly, Blake and Haddie were snatched by their collars. But it wasn't Farmer Don.

Big enamel cow teeth opened wide as two cows scooped up the kids without missing a stride. Pointing their tails and their ears straight back didn't help much. Cows are slow even when they are streamlined.

Three cows, two cow kids, and one mad cowboy running for town. What a sight! They ran right down the middle of Main Street just as the big annual Homecoming Parade started! They plowed through the police, passed up the posse, flew by the floats, and chugged by the cheerleaders. The crowd shouted and yelled and clapped. The parade ended at the school house. There were hundreds of students cheering from the bleachers, and the mayor was at the podium boring all the intellectual high school teachers!

Everyone slid to a stop. Jumping gracefully from the podium, Mayor Eunice Dee Clark announced, "Udderly delightful! Oh, what a lark! First place!"

She hung fancy blue ribbons from the proud cows' necks. The cows did that big "cow smile" thing again! The mayor handed Blake an envelope that read HOMECOMING PARADE — FIRST PLACE. Everyone stood and cheered and clapped.

Farmer Don turned to the mayor who was still clapping and said, "I had these here cows sold at the stockyards fer 500 bucks and these kids are stealing cows right out of trucks! I want 'em arrested and I want ma cows back."

The mayor laughed and clapped some more. She thought it was part of their act for the parade. As he sat on the cow's wide back, Blake opened the envelope marked FIRST PLACE.

Inside were five one-hundred-dollar bills.

Blake handed the money to Farmer Don. As he counted every bill, the crowd grew perfectly still. He stuffed the money into his pocket, tipped his hat to the mayor, and winked at the children.

Walking into the sunset, old Farmer Don looked rather charming as he announced, "Might jist take up chicken farmin'."

When the celebrities got home, Dad and Mom greeted them with wide-open arms at the gate. The cows gave Dad a big cow smile, and Dad gave them a big COW smile right back.

And so you see, everything in life isn't BLACK AND WHITE!

Often there are heroes who do what is right!

Hence, our tale ends in udder delight!

THE END

Always Be Kind to Animals

Always be kind to animals,
Morning, noon, and night;
For animals have feelings too,
And furthermore, they bite.

John Gardner